Milton Grant hated other people's bad habits. His life
was spiralling out of control, and he decided to begin
a symbolic correction programme. A chance event in
a supermarket lit his fuse, and it became apparent that
people were going to die.

Inspired by the Michael Douglas film *Falling Down*.

The Man Who Hated

by

Tony Drury

Novella
Nostalgia

Published by City Fiction

ISBN: 978-1-910040-18-8

THE MAN WHO HATED

He was trapped, and she was the cause.

There were knobbly joints in Elsie's fingers. The cartilage had become pitted and brittle and she could not straighten them. She had been late that morning in taking her analgesics. The young woman on the supermarket till was patient, sympathetic and told her customer to take all the time she needed. The eighty-year-old had some vouchers which could reduce her bill. She managed to find them in her purse, which was at the bottom of her bag. There were nine, but three were out of date. Frustration flashed across her face because she did not have enough cash to pay for the seven items on the conveyor belt. Elsie looked around. She needed to use the toilet.

Three of the purchases were frozen meals. They were a treat for the weekend ahead. She told the assistant she would have to pay with her credit card which was in her coat pocket, but she could not remember which one. The young woman suggested that she try the right-hand side, and there it was. Slowly, Elsie managed to push the card into the slot. She could not recall the PIN but then she remembered: it was her birthday. 1934. She briefly relived her early years in pre-war Brighton. Agonisingly, she pressed the four digits: 1934. 1 August 1934. The card was rejected. Elsie looked up and apologised for being a silly old woman.

Milton Grant concurred: he was due to have sex at

eleven-thirty. He had completed his shopping and selected this particular till because the customer being served only had a few items in her basket. As he laid out his organic purchases, a woman with two children came in behind him and started to add her groceries behind his purchases. The customer at the front of the queue was taking ages to complete her business. Milton was pleased she had such disfigured hands. He hoped her painkillers were not strong enough to provide more than temporary relief.

He made eye contact with the checkout assistant. She immediately looked away. Her hand hovered over the call button as she wondered if he was going to kick off. The situation was frustrating, but her training had emphasised that every customer was important. She was reassured by his shrug and casual glance at his watch. His benign expression concealed his loathing and impatience.

He hated his name: Milton. He had instigated several fights at school when mates tried to shorten it to Milt. His patriotic parents, before they separated, had named him after a new town in Buckinghamshire. This was post-war Britain and people were full of hope and ambition. The government was building hundreds of new homes in a place called Milton Keynes. Stella liked his name. If he satisfied her in the way she relished, she would say, "Milton, that was heaven." It was a pity about the other matter...

The supermarket assistant suggested that her customer tried the PIN one more time. Elsie pressed 1934. It was rejected. Milton felt tension in his stomach. The woman behind him was telling her children how much she loved them. His anger was mounting. The older woman cried out: she remembered she had read an article in the *Daily Mail* about credit card security and she had reversed her birth year for her PIN to make it safer. Elsie entered in 3491 and it was rejected. The assistant suggested that the reverse was 4391. The elderly lady laughed and said, "Silly me, dear." Milton was just about holding his temper. Elsie entered 4391 and the assistant celebrated the completion of the transaction with her. Elsie put the credit card into her pocket, thanked the young woman on the till, picked up her shopping and immediately dropped the bag. Two of the six eggs smashed.

It took around four minutes to clean the floor. By this time, the customer behind Milton was struggling to control her children. The earlier theme of matriarchal love had been replaced by bribes as she opened a packet of chocolate biscuits and reluctantly distributed them. She told Milton she was in a hurry and blinked when she heard his reply. The till cleared and he paid for his purchases, rather abruptly indicating he did not want cash back. He hurried away for his eleven-thirty appointment.

As he drove out of the supermarket car park, he spotted the old lady hobbling towards the bus stop. Elsie was unsteady on her feet, which pleased him. He waited his moment and slowly drove alongside her. As she glanced towards his vehicle, he suddenly pulled over towards her. She threw her arms into the air and fell onto her right side, crashing into a concrete bollard and screaming as her femur shattered.

Milton laughed as he drove away. He knew that his car's registration number was being recorded on the CCTV. That would not help the police in any way.

3

The vehicle had false plates. Tomorrow, he would drive to Shoreditch in East London where he would meet a man he had once arrested for car theft. Milton would buy a replacement vehicle from him for cash. He'd then drive the forty miles home, garage his vehicle and fit new number plates.

It was eleven twenty-nine when he pulled up in her drive. Their ritual remained unchanged. After he had taken early retirement from his job as a police constable, having convinced the medical authorities that the demands of attending motorway accidents was resulting in stress and loss of sleep, he divorced his wife and told his daughter, Jennifer, that he would send her three hundred pounds every month. His plan was taking shape. At last his life had a point to it. He met Stella on a dating website, having paid five hundred pounds for the introduction. Hers was the twenty-third reply he had received; he had rejected the gold-diggers and one woman he suspected of plotting an entrapment. The site had a feature he liked. People could connect but were not allowed to share photographs. Milton knew exactly how to get around that, but he played by the rules because he liked Stella's candid answers. Stella had been through two divorces and was concerned about becoming involved with another potential husband. She was not prepared to risk the humiliation of a third failed relationship, but let slip that her two former spouses had funded her future needs. Her sons had long since left home, but they stayed in touch from Estonia and the Antarctic.

They met. Milton looked after himself by following a near-vegetarian diet and taking daily six-mile runs. He also went hillwalking regularly, where he relished the solitude of the peaks. Stella worked part-time in a local hospital as a physiotherapist. She knew she was a few pounds overweight, but was fairly secure that her attraction to men remained potent. She was sexually intuitive and, within three meetings, had Milton summed up, ready for the bedroom. Sex was straightforward: he was a normal heterosexual male. He had no special requirements; he loved female flesh and reacted positively when it was revealed, sensitively. During their second meeting, in a coffee shop, he told her that he occasionally watched *Breakfast at Tiffany's* so that he could enjoy the scene in the Manhattan flat where Audrey Hepburn playfully messes around in a white shirt, allowing the revelation of her near-perfect figure.

Stella greeted him at the door with a glass of pinot grigio. They pecked each other's cheek and shared a few minutes together drinking the wine. She made a comment about his punctuality and followed up with her usual mannerism. Milton wished she wouldn't, but let it go. They went into the back room extension, where their privacy was assured. She had prepared the Jacuzzi ready for their time together: she had saved up for it and she loved it.

She was wearing a long pink shirt. They sat down by the Jacuzzi and sipped a second glass of wine. Stella crossed her legs but ensured that the material did not rise up above her thighs. Her skin was smooth, and the undoing of a top button revealed more of it to Milton. They exchanged small talk, discussing politics and the rise of Jeremy Corbyn. Milton suggested that the slogan 'For the many, not the few' brilliantly caught the mood of the country. She teased him by telling him she found the Labour leader rather sexy. She uncrossed her legs, allowing the shirt to rise a little. He wondered what she might reveal next. Stella had chosen black knickers because she had worked out the colour stirred his juices. She lifted her bottom off the seat and pulled the shirt from under her, leaning over to test the temperature of the water. She stood up and encouraged Milton to stand too. She undressed him and led him to the steps. As he submerged himself, she removed her shirt. Two hours later she sighed with pleasure. "Milton," she said, "that was heaven."

Milton left her house around three in the afternoon and went to the cinema to see *American Assassin*, which he found entertaining. He related to the vengeful CIA black ops recruit Mitch Rapp as he helped a Cold War veteran (Michael Keaton) stop the detonation of a nuclear device. The brooding Shiva Negar, playing the mysterious Annika, took his fancy. When she was being tortured in a bath tub it made him wonder about Stella's Jacuzzi and its potential for excitement. He left the cinema, bought a vegetarian pizza, returned home and opened a bottle of chilled white wine which he took into his office. Milton switched on a CD of Chopin études, which added to his contentment. He and his companion met twice weekly and occasionally went out for Sunday lunch. He liked her… but he wished she wouldn't do that one thing.

He had wondered whether to tell her about his mission – especially as she occasionally chided him for having few outside interests – but he decided not to, chastising himself for showing weakness. Secrecy was paramount, and he had no wish to even be interviewed by the police. He looked at his list of eighteen possible corrections and eight situations. This was the result of many weeks of research of people's pet hates. The difference was that he, Milton Grant, would do something about it instead of just moaning. He and Stella would have Sunday lunch together and he would start his mission on Tuesday, in the knowledge that she would be waiting for him in the afternoon.

He had selected 'traffic lights' as his first correction, remembering the case as though it had only happened yesterday. He had been a police officer for five years, on traffic duty, when he was called to a minor collision. The lights had turned from amber to green and the lady driver and her companion, who had turned to face each other, had continued their conversation, ignoring the horns from the two cars behind them. One driver got out and went to remonstrate with the driver, who reacted angrily then accelerated away, not noticing that the lights had changed to red. A van hit her.

Milton had arrived at the scene to see three people shouting at each other. The woman driver then collapsed. A paramedic arrived and she was taken to hospital. The Crown Prosecution Service prosecuted her for driving without due care and attention. She asked for the advice of her husband, who suggested that one of Lincoln's Inn's finest criminal barristers should defend her. Milton was confident about the evidence he would give until, under pressure from the defence counsel, he made a comment about women needing to face each other when they were talking.

He was only repeating what the driver behind the defendant's car had told him.

Counsel pounced and managed to discredit his evidence, believing he was prejudiced against women drivers. The case was dismissed, the CPS lawyer called Milton a moron and, as he left the court, the woman came up and thanked him for being a misogynist.

This event had coincided with Milton's growing realisation that his wife and young daughter were establishing an alliance which resulted in an unhealthy accusation of his perceived faults. He decided to have a vasectomy as he wanted no more children. His wife found out when she opened the bill from the hospital – and that, effectively, was that. They struggled on for another few years until her parents died within a few months of each other. She inherited half a house and bought out her brother. Their divorce was business-like and Milton breathed a sigh of relief when he finally gained his independence.

The seeds of his correction programme, in which he had decided to make an example of people guilty of eight of the worst faults he had detected in his fellow human beings, had been sown both by his experiences as a police officer and on receiving the diagnosis from his doctor. He would carry out the first correction next Tuesday. The first on the list, 'traffic lights', was one that annoyed him beyond expression, although several others were equally irritating. After the court case he had found himself becoming obsessed by drivers who were slow to react when traffic lights turned green. With the increasing number of vehicles on the roads, it was selfish for drivers to take too long to accelerate away from traffic lights. He spent Friday travelling down to London to meet his acquaintance, change his car and replace the number plates. Stella joined him for Sunday lunch at a local pub. They discussed his love of classical piano music and her obsession with *Strictly Come Dancing*. She knew her Chopin, but was annoyed by the results of the voting from the previous evening's programme.

By Tuesday morning Milton had put on two stone in weight, lost his hair and was two inches taller. His inspiration for this disguise was the Clint Eastwood film *In the Line of Fire*. In it, actor John Malkovich played the part of Mitch Leary, the former Secret Service agent who told the President's personal security officer that he was going to kill his boss. He plagued Clint Eastwood by continually disguising himself. Milton had watched the film time and again and revelled in the finale, in which Agent Frank Horrigan (played by Eastwood) dived in front of the President and took the bullet fired by Mitch Leary. He also won the heart of Agent Lily Raines (played by Rene Russo), whose bedroom antics and black underwear left Milton Grant dripping with sweat.

After spending several hours perfecting fitting his range of hairpieces, he swallowed a small piece of cordite which was an army technique to make the skin temporarily go white. He padded out a jacket two sizes too big for him and put on platform shoes. On Monday he travelled to some local woods which he explored to ensure he was familiar with them. After leaving his car at home, he went indoors, changed his clothes and walked half a mile to the garage he rented, carrying a suitcase. This was where he kept the vehicle he had bought in Shoreditch the previous Friday, and which now had false number plates. He stored his disguise in the boot. He went to bed early, slept soundly and woke up early, whereupon he went for a six-mile run followed by a shower and a breakfast of mixed nuts, raisins and fresh fruit.

He wanted to find his victim in the Tuesday morning commuter traffic. At around eight-fifteen there would be a combination of office workers and school-run parents fighting for space at the crossroads he had selected. He was not fussed if his victim was male, female or even transgender, although he abhorred all the modern nonsense about LGBT. He just wanted to find an example of a selfish driver failing to respond to the changing lights in a considerate manner.

He collected his car from the garage and parked in a side street, then walked to the traffic lights and took up position. As he stood there, a youth in a Vauxhall Astra delayed accelerating away due to the fact he was resetting his iPod. He was oblivious to the protests behind him and, having found the music of his choice, sat up and checked his acne in the driver's mirror, brushing away the flecks of dead skin. The van driver behind him gave another angry wake-up blow of his horn. After looking in his mirror, the Astra driver lowered his window and held out his hand, his middle finger pointing in the air. He refocused on the lights, which were changing from amber to red, accelerated away and left several frustrated drivers behind him.

Milton rushed to his car, turned into the main road, spotted the red Astra ahead of him, and was following it when the driver turned into a private car park for employees of the local council. Milton drove on, parked in a side street and waited for an hour before returning to search for the red Astra, using the registration number he had written down. He found it towards the back of the parking area. He was glad the car park had no security. Taking out a portable drill he punctured the four tyres, found his tube of transparent glue and sealed all the locks and handles. He took out a plastic container and smeared oil over the windscreen. Then he stuffed mashed cardboard into the exhaust pipe. After ducking for cover when an employee of the council came to collect her car, he decided that she had not seen him, waited for several minutes and then stood up. Taking out a piece of white paper, he applied some glue and plastered it onto the oily windscreen. When the car driver had returned to his car, recovered from his shock, then removed the adhesive from the locks, changed his tyres, sat down in his seat and looked ahead he would read:

When the lights change to green, it means you drive away as quickly and safely as possible.

The driver would later discover the consequences of a blocked exhaust pipe.

Milton parked in Stella's driveway and immediately accepted the offered glass of champagne, making his way into the hall. The white shirt she was wearing was frustratingly opaque. Her skin glistened. They exchanged small talk, and her mannerism appeared briefly. He just wished she wouldn't do it. In the back room, the lights from the hot tub provided the only illumination. Sniffing the air, he sighed with sensual pleasure. She had strategically placed a series of Hooyei-koh incense sticks around the room. The

Japanese 'Eternal Treasure' was giving off a mixture of sandalwood and cinnamon. They would burn for around an hour. Long before that Milton would be submerged in the water. Perhaps two hours later he would be receiving the reassurance that their time together had been "heaven".

Police Constable Lucy Smith threw a peanut at her husband, Detective Sergeant David Smith. He was universally known as Dave, apart from to his mother, to whom he was David. His mother had originally worried about the nine-year age difference between her son and his new wife but, two years on, all seemed to be well. It needed to be. Police marriages were notoriously unstable, but she was reassured when she read in a magazine that statistics revealed that police officers who married another police officer generally experienced more fulfilling relationships than officers who found partners outside the police force.

Dave looked up. "I said no, and I mean no."

"I've a cold bottle of lager in the fridge for you," said Lucy.

"Anything else on offer?" asked her libidinous husband.

"How about a cold bottle of lager from the fridge?" replied Lucy.

He laughed. Dave could not believe his luck: his wife was scrumptious.

"Luce," he said. "We agreed, no work gossip at home."

"You also promised a number of other things at the altar," she laughed.

"That was to impress your mother," he said.

She returned from the kitchen with the bribe.

"I'll give you two sentences," he said.

"OK then," she began. "This one is really strange. A man, who we have on CCTV but can't identify, goes into a car park owned by the council and vandalises a car. He punctures all the tyres, glues the locks, puts oil on the windscreen and stuffs mashed cardboard into the exhaust."

Dave held out his empty glass and gave her a pleading look. She stood up, moved towards the kitchen and returned with another glass of lager. Lucy knew she might appear to be a subservient wife, but to hell with gender equality. She knew that Dave loved her and she was happy with their relationship. And what was to happen within weeks would reveal her inner strength...

"You drink too much," she chided. "You're beginning to get a paunch."

"I know a way to lose that..." he said.

"Later." Lucy smiled. "You said two sentences. Well, having trashed the car he left a message on the windscreen."

"Call Patel Car Valeting Services on...." chuckled Dave.

"It read *When the lights change to green, it means you drive away as quickly and safely as possible.*"

"I can only imagine that the owner was none too pleased," Dave commented.

"You mean 'call me Dowie'," said Lucy. "He was incensed. It didn't stop him trying to look down my blouse." She sipped her glass of elderflower. "When I asked him if anyone had any reason to bear a grudge against him, such as an ex-girlfriend, he gave me fifteen names then stopped."

"So, why are you telling me this in breach of our marital vows?" said Dave.

"It's not one of his exes, Dave."

"Ah. So now we are a detective," Dave said.

Lucy had moved over to sit at his feet.

"I'm in my second month of secondment," she said. "I really do want to be a detective constable."

"No one was hurt. The police don't care about cars any more. It doesn't help the statistics. Move on, Luce," suggested her husband.

Lucy stood up and went to look out of the window. "And if it was your case, Dave, would you move on?"

"No," he replied.

"Ah ha!" cried Lucy. "Why not, Detective Sergeant Smith?"

"Because of the exhaust pipe," he replied.

"The exhaust pipe?" she exclaimed.

"You are saying he stuffed mashed cardboard into the exhaust pipe," he said.

"Yes, Dave. The engineer said—"

"Luce. Trust me. Whoever he is, he's nasty."

Criminally, the engineer had failed to clear all the mashed cardboard out of the exhaust pipe. A section had been pushed further inside and had hardened. Dowie had finally been able to collect his vehicle, and spent a long time returning it to its pristine condition to attract the girls.

He was furious that someone had vandalised his precious car, and needed to assuage his anger. He drove to the motorway feeder road and accelerated away. He checked his hair in the mirror, chuffed with the high fade and textured quiff which his pal in The

Razor Sharp Salon had done for free. Dowie turned on the music and began to croon.

Within the car engine, pressure was building as discarded gases built up inside the exhaust system. Finally, the head gasket blew. The car rapidly lost power and slowed down in the outside lane. Dowie banged his foot down on the accelerator pedal, looked in his mirror and saw a lorry bearing down on him. Panicking, he opened the car door and flung himself out of the stationary vehicle. He landed on the central crash barrier and slumped, screaming, to the ground on the other side. This protected him from the carnage as the lorry, the driver blaring his horn, smashed into his car, demolishing it.

The music filling his office reflected his mood. Milton was elated by the success of his first correction, and relished the thought of the selfish motorist trying to sort out his vandalised car. As Milton absorbed the uncharacteristically cheerful music of Dimitri Shostakovich, who had dedicated his Piano Concerto no. 2 in F major to his son Maxim on his nineteenth birthday, Milton thought about Stella, who had been at her sensual best. Thursday could not come soon enough.

Milton looked down at his list. He had taken an item from the reserve page and added it to his total of eight human faults. It was now at number two. The incident had taken place two hours earlier. The odour had nauseated him. It must have occurred on the grassy area between his driveway and the road. As he entered his hall he looked down and realised that his carpet was smeared with dog mess. Tearing off his shoes, although only the right one was affected, he rushed into the kitchen, took out a plastic bin liner, threw the shoes into it, went outside through the side entrance, soaked his feet and threw the waste into the dustbin. He returned to his kitchen, took off his clothes, prepared a bucket full of soapy water, went back into the hall and scrubbed and scrubbed until the carpet was free of any canine waste. Back in the kitchen, he poured the contents of the bucket down the sink, disinfected the whole area and went upstairs and put on his running kit. He left his house and ran for six miles, returning soaked to the skin. He stripped off and showered. He dried himself, dressed in casual clothes, entered his office, put on his chosen music and began to plan correction number two.

During his years as a police constable human behaviour had often perplexed him. He had been called to a block of twelve flats in a pleasant suburban area. Eleven of the homes were occupied by a mixture of law-abiding citizens (well, relatively – two were involved in tax fiddles and one abused his wife) who wanted to sleep at night. The twelfth, a man in his fifties, played David Bowie's music, rather too loudly, throughout the night. Every night. In the end, at considerable cost to the taxpayer, the council managed to obtain an order against him. The music lover moved half a mile into another block of flats and repeated the same pattern of behaviour.

As far as Milton was concerned, dog shit came into the same category of selfishness. It baffled him that a minority of owners refused to clear up after their pet. How could they desecrate public areas where children played? The law of the land was clear. The Public Spaces Protection Order stipulated that dogs must be kept on a lead, they were not allowed in restricted places (such as farmland), and the owner must clear up after his animal had defecated. Inevitably, a minority decided that they were above the law.

It took him the whole of Wednesday to prepare his corrective campaign. He walked for miles with a plastic scoop and bucket. By the end of the day he was ready. As always, sleep came easily. In the morning, he woke refreshed, ran six miles, showered and ate breakfast. The morning would be spent in the local park, where he might be vulnerable to being caught on CCTV. This was countered with a simple disguise. He wore a hat, put on glasses with clear lenses, carried a walking stick and assumed a limp. Adding an indistinctive raincoat, dark trousers and black shoes, he carried his equipment in a supermarket carrier bag.

By nine o'clock, after the school run was over, he was in the local park. His plan went well – until it went wrong. He kept to the tree line and watched for dog walkers who did not clear up their pet's mess. By ten-thirty he had located and punished three offenders. After each had committed the offence, he followed them until the opportunity came for him to slip into their pocket – or, preferably, the bag they were carrying – a plain envelope. When his first victim returned home, she groomed her cocker spaniel and then discovered the package in her shopping bag. It was not sealed. She undid the flap and put her hand inside, recoiling as she felt the sticky substance into which she had placed her fingers. She pulled it out and felt ill as it dawned on her what it was. The dog owner read the notice she had withdrawn from the envelope:

You selfish person. Clean your dog's mess up. Look at your fingers. A child could have landed in your animal's poo. I'll be watching you.

She ran to the toilet and vomited, then afterwards vowed never again to fail to collect her pet's mess.

The fourth candidate for correction proved to have a different attitude. There was a car park near the lake. Milton was resting at the water's edge, eating an apple. He saw a middle-aged man get out of his Range Rover, open the rear door and release a bloodhound. It did not go too far before stopping and emptying its bowels in the middle of the path. There seemed to be a mountain of excrement. The owner whistled and walked away in the opposite direction. Milton watched with growing anger. He waited for a few moments as several walkers skirted round the mess, then went over and scooped the whole pile into his bag, having taken out the remaining envelopes. Returning to the dog owner's car, he smeared the shit all over the windscreen. He took out one of the notices and placed it in the centre of the screen, hid in the trees and waited.

The owner returned twenty minutes later, opened the rear door and encouraged the bloodhound to jump into the boot. He went round to the front of his vehicle and looked at the message, lifted it off and read it. He laughed, went back to the rear door and opened it. Taking out some rags and an ice scraper he proceeded to clear the windscreen, whistling as he did so. He put the cleaning items back in the car and then, to Milton's complete surprise, gave a command. Out jumped a small mongrel. The man then closed and locked the vehicle. The second pet ran away, then stopped and defecated on the path. The owner whistled and walked off in the opposite direction again. Milton followed him.

His opportunity came a few minutes later when the dog owner sat down on a park bench and stared across the lake. Milton checked the area and saw there was nobody around. Approaching the dog walker from behind, he hit him across the back of the neck with a fallen branch. He then put his arm around the dazed man and, with his right hand, smeared excrement all over his face, squeezing closed his victim's nostrils. As the dog walker gasped for breath, Milton stuffed shit into his mouth. He whispered into his ear, "Got the message, arsehole?"

Lucy and Dave were reluctant to accept mid-week invitations. Working at different police stations (Dave was attached to Area HQ) gave them problems when trying to co-ordinate their hours. This Wednesday evening, however, they were both off, and they were sitting around a dinner table with Annabel and Amjit. Both were doctors at different local practices. Annabel's friendship with Lucy had originated at high school. As they opened the third bottle of wine (with Lucy on Diet Coke and driving duty), the conversation became more excitable. Annabel and Amjit had been to Glastonbury and were reliving some of the music of Foo Fighters – although Annabel would have preferred Jamie Cullum who, for her, had lit up the weekend. The hosts asked about Lucy and Dave's police work. This often happened on social occasions. Dave was a past master at deflecting the subject. Lucy, who was clear-headed, asked to be excused and returned a few moments later looking ashen. Dave failed to understand the signs. Annabel did, and she put her hand on Lucy's arm and encouraged her friend to talk.

"We're not allowed to talk about what we do," said Lucy.

"So what's happened?" asked Annabel. "I've been your friend for a long time. You're a tough one. Something's upset you. What is it?"

"Luce," said Dave, "shall we go home?"

"It sounds awful," said Lucy. "He stuffed dog poo into his mouth."

She stood up and rushed to the toilet. Amjit followed her. A few minutes later they were all together again around the table. Annabel served coffee. Lucy told the whole story: the emergency call from the park, the taking of the victim into hospital following his violent allergic reaction, the police search of the area, the forensic team working on the notice, and the reaction of the man's wife, who wanted to sue everybody.

"Luce. Tell us again. What did the notice say?"

Lucy was now recovering her poise. "*You selfish person. Clean your dog's mess up. Look at your fingers. A child could have landed in your animal's poo. I'll be watching you.*"

"That's nasty," said Annabel as she kissed her friend.

As they drove home, David had a deep frown on his face.

"Please stop the car, Lucy," he asked.

She did as requested and came to a halt in a lay-by. She turned and faced her husband.

"I'm very sorry, Dave. I'll never do it again. I was totally out of order."

He hugged his wife and suggested they went home.

Lucy began to drive away.

"Dave," she said, "did you hear the word that Annabel used?"

"What word?"

"She said 'nasty'." She slowed and indicated to pass a cyclist, then accelerated away. "Nasty," she said again, rather quietly.

Milton turned up the volume as he prepared to listen to Rachmaninov's Piano Concerto no. 1 in F sharp minor. He slumped at his desk, the list in his hand. Using an orange marker pen, he eliminated 'traffic lights' and 'dog poo'. The 'vivace' came and went and the pianist slowed to begin the 'andante'. He sipped a whisky. With six subjects to go, he knew which would be number eight. It was the one that best summed up the demented – or perhaps tormented – person he was becoming.

He returned to the selection process. There were seven minutes remaining of the 'allegro vivace' in which to make up his mind. The acid mixture was ready. It was no contest. He marked his list with 'No. 3' by the chosen category. He would do it on Tuesday and then he'd see Stella in the afternoon. He was excited by the thought of what was to come. He spent the next four days alone.

On Saturday, Stella phoned Milton to excuse herself from Sunday lunch, explaining she'd decided to run an extra physiotherapy surgery as she had so many patients waiting for an appointment. Easing her patients' symptoms was the easy part of her job. Sorting out the causes of their problems was more of a challenge – and the responsibility of doctors and surgeons. She knew, both as a human being and as a

21

professional, that around half her patients were overweight. In a five-minute examination of a near naked person she would nearly always diagnose the cause of their problems but she would never judge; that was not her role. Earlier that day she had watched her patient, a man in his fifties, crawl to the weighing scales. He weighed in at twenty-two stones, and told Stella he had been a big baby. Later in the session she asked him about his diet – and how many beers he consumed in an average day. His answers were complete fabrications.

She told Milton about this, and was more than surprised by his reaction.

"Fucking selfish bastards," he suggested. "They know they're fat. They make ludicrous excuses and then expect society to provide for them. Some people are so fat they're stuck in their own houses, and the ambulance service has to get hoists made to get them out." He paused. "Stella, why do we pussyfoot round? Tell them straight. 'You're fat. Lose some fucking weight. If you don't, we'll leave you at the side of the road'."

"And who makes that judgement, Milton?" she asked.

"The ambulance crew. There are enough people who genuinely need their help," he said.

"Yes, I get your drift, but who do you take to hospital and who do you leave by the side of the road?"

"It always the same claptrap, Stella." He sighed. "I'm talking sense and you're going to tell me about their human rights."

"No, I'm bloody not," she said, raising her voice. "Don't you think I feel the same as you? Do you have any idea what it's like physically trying to massage an obese person?"

"Exactly! Throw them out and concentrate on the ones who can be of use to society."

"Milton," she responded angrily, "that's obscene."

"Is it?" he snapped. "Perhaps I'm one of the few people prepared to think the unthinkable."

"You don't get it, do you?" She wiped her eyes. "I'm asking you, who makes the choice? 'Just a moment, Mr Brown, I'll be with you in a moment and we'll sort out your back pain.' 'Sorry, Mr Robinson, you're fat and over twenty stones. We're going to leave you in a field.'"

"So answer me this. Truthfully, please. Are you seeing more and more obese people?"

She put her head in her hands and slumped forward. "I've now got twelve children under ten years old who are more than 70% over their correct weight." She sighed. "The truth is, Milton, we don't know what to do about it."

"You know that everybody has a view about the NHS, Stella?" he asked.

"Oh yes." She laughed.

"Do you know what the NHS's real problem is?"

"Money," she answered. "We are low down the European scale for spending per patient as a percentage of GDP." She looked pleased with her reply.

"No," responded Milton.

"All right, then, tell me," she said.

"The NHS has created its own problem."

"Problem?" she repeated.

"It's too successful at keeping people alive. Whereas they used to nurse people in their seventies, patients today are mostly in their eighties."

"Good point," said Stella.

"That's not the challenge," he continued.

"So what is?" Stella asked, increasingly frustrated.

"People in their eighties are more fragile and vulnerable. The NHS is taking care of an increasingly demanding age group. They fill hospital beds, they need many more prescriptions, they need surgery, and their relatives laugh all the way to their sun-filled beaches as the taxpayer picks up all the bills."

"Yes and no," said Stella.

Milton stared at her.

"Some of the relatives I meet are saints. Without their commitment to their relatives – usually their elderly parents – hospitals would collapse." She hesitated. "But you're right. We have whole wards full of people needing full-time care, and their children have simply walked away."

"Blocking A&E departments," he added.

"Milton. I can solve this," said Stella.

"Go for it," he encouraged.

"Pass a new law. When UK residents reach eighty years of age, they are exiled to a Pacific island."

Milton stared at her. "Brilliant!" he exclaimed. "Just my style."

She noticed that he wasn't laughing.

He looked at her, thoughtfully. "Of course, a neater solution would be to shoot them."

Milton always slept soundly now he had a bed to himself. Two days later he woke at 6am, put on his running shorts and shirt, shuddered as he opened the side door and felt the chill autumn wind, and began his six-mile run which would take him round the local park. He returned within his forty-seven-minute target, showered and put on his tracksuit, omitting breakfast because he could not risk any stomach upset. After sipping some water, he left the house carrying a green bag. He went into his garage, where he had assembled his equipment. He stripped off and took out the clothes he had bought in several London stores. The bra strap caught his skin and he winced as he adjusted it. The silk knickers might have suggested a bizarre sexual desire. Their purpose was rather different: it was necessary to think like a woman. He knew he would be picked up by CCTV and possible witnesses, and he needed to convey the image and personality of a female. It had taken him over three hours in Oxford Street to achieve the appearance he wanted. He had bought the coat from a charity shop. He checked himself in the full-length mirror he had smuggled into the garage. He wore flat sandals, knowing he'd have to change the way he walked and take shorter strides to pass for a woman. The weather forecast predicted a chilly but dry day. It was a thirty-two-mile journey to the centre of the nearby town. At seven forty-five he was in place – and ready to select his first victim.

And there she was. He disliked her the moment he set eyes on her, because she epitomised the selfishness of the modern phone user. She had come out of the railway station and was walking towards the office block at the end of the road. "You bitch," he said quietly to himself as he watched other commuters skirt around her as she strolled, eyes down, glued to her mobile phone. She was immaculately dressed and she seemed to be sending a text message. An older man stepped out of her path into the road, and a cyclist shouted at him.

Milton made a quick calculation. He realised that if he cut through the shopping mall he could possibly overtake her and then turn back. His manoeuvres worked well and within three minutes he was walking towards her down a quieter street. He froze as he saw that she still had her fucking mobile held out in front of her – and now she was laughing. The woman passed close to him, fully occupied by her phone. She never noticed the plastic barrel protruding out of the side of his coat. She didn't notice him squeeze the plastic bulb in his hand. She did not immediately register the acid as it smeared over the inner side of her left thigh. The mixture Milton had prepared contained a slow-acting constituent to give him a few moments to leave the scene.

She stumbled and dropped her phone. Her leg went from beneath her and she fell to the pavement. She started to scream, writhing in agony. A man rushed over to her.

"Are you OK?" he asked. "What happened?"

"My leg! My leg!" she yelled as the tears poured down her face.

He moved her coat and gasped as he saw the mess the acid had made of her limb. He pulled out his phone to call the emergency services. Her phone lay on the pavement.

The paramedics arrived within minutes and immediately listed the case as urgent. She was rushed to hospital. In the coming two years she was to undergo thirteen operations – and would wear jeans for the rest of her life, to avoid the stares of other people.

Three hours later Milton had attacked five more

people. It was proving more difficult than he had anticipated, partly because of increased police activity and because he was careful to select deserving victims. When he finally returned to his car he had assaulted another four women and a man. He drove towards the motorway, stopped at the pre-selected section of the woods, walked for a mile, changed his clothes and buried the bag containing his female disguise deep in the undergrowth. Milton walked back to his car and drove to Shoreditch, where he sold his car and bought a van. Then he returned to his garage and changed the number plates. He reached Stella a little after four o'clock. She did not ask why he was later than usual. Their routine remained unchanged, although she found him tense and taut. The wine, the hot tub and scented water, the striptease and the caressing were delivered in their usual way and he responded with his usual vigour, but then found he couldn't reach orgasm.

She laughed and he hated the sound.

He finally achieved climax, then quickly dressed and reassured her that he was well satisfied. He just wished she wouldn't do it.

Lucy was running around the lounge of their modest home, waving a yellow card in the air.

"Yellow card," she said, laughing. "Dave Smith is awarded a yellow card for trying to begin shop talk, contrary to our marriage vows."

"Luce," he pleaded, "not tonight, love. Please, not tonight. I've had a terrible day."

She entered the kitchen and poured him a glass of lager, quickly returning and putting it into his hand. He nodded his appreciation of her understanding as she sat opposite him.

"I'm sorry, love. What's happened?" she asked.

"Didn't you hear it on the news?"

"I've been studying all afternoon," she responded. "Want to talk about it?"

"No."

She pulled her legs underneath her and sat very still.

"Some bastard's been spraying acid on innocent people," he said.

"Shit," said Lucy.

"Six attacks in three hours, Luce." He drank deeply. "In the centre of town," he continued. "Two badly injured, four others hurt."

"CCTV?" asked Lucy.

"We've got her," he said. "A middle-aged woman carrying a tube which she hid inside her coat. She sprayed people as she went past them."

"So arrest her," suggested Lucy.

"We can't find her," Dave responded. "We've had every single available officer out today. You couldn't drop a sweet paper without being arrested. She just disappeared." He paused. "Luce?"

She stood up and went over to her husband, sat on his lap and kissed him.

"Go on, tell me, Dave," she said. "You'll feel better if you get it off your chest."

"Luce," he said and then choked. "There's nothing I haven't seen in my career. Abused babies, motorway carnage and the rest." He wiped his eyes. "The first victim. She's nineteen, absolutely beautiful and, until this morning, had her whole life ahead of her. But her thigh was eaten away by the acid down to the bone. It was hideous."

"She'll still have a life ahead of her, Dave," she said. "An abused baby usually has nothing."

"Yes, you're right." He sighed. "I suppose it's because I can hide my emotions with a battered child: there's usually nothing I can do. This woman, today... it was awful to see a life with such potential destroyed."

"Dave," said Lucy, "I want you to go upstairs and shower. When you come down I will have prepared some nibbles and opened another bottle of lager. I want you to tell me everything." As he stood up, she hugged him.

An hour later Dave had told her everything. Lucy listened attentively. She was staggered by the amount of information the police had obtained. In each of the six attacks, the victims were minding their own business, thinking about their lives, taking calls, in one case catching a train, or planning to stop for coffee. The man was going for a job interview. The attacks were clearly random and, beyond hurting the individuals, seemingly inexplicable. The acid had already been analysed and an initial report suggested a professional attacker was at large. A team was watching hours of CCTV for clues, and the woman had been captured no less than seventeen times. Unfortunately, she apparently knew the system and had tried hard to ensure her face was not visible so she could not be identified. They talked until nearly eleven-thirty. Then they went to bed and held each other closely. Dave was soon snoring. At two-thirty Lucy was shaking her husband, trying to wake him.

"Dave!" she was shouting. "Wake up!"

Slowly, he focused.

"What is it?"

"Dave," she cried. "They were all using mobile phones. That's what they had in common!"

He shot up in bed.

"We need to talk about this. I'll make a pot of tea," he said.

He was back within four minutes and poured himself a cup in his Arsenal mug. He wore a deep frown.

"Luce. You're inspirational. And you're right. All of them were using mobiles. The two sisters were texting each other: crazy."

"So their heads were down," said Lucy.

"And so they didn't see the attacker approach them," he continued. "That was clear from the CCTV."

"But she saw them," said Lucy.

Dave frowned. "That's where we drew a blank," he said.

"Dave," said Lucy, but she did not wait for a response. "I'm not yet a detective." She paused as her husband went to say something. "No. Let me finish. Criminal work is for you men, while we PCs help old ladies across the street."

"Don't be too hard on yourself, Luce," he said and chuckled. "So?"

"So, what if I tried some detective work?"

"You were saying about helping old ladies across the street," he laughed.

"Nasty," she said.

"Sorry, Luce. Just trying to be funny."

"That's what you said when I asked you about the man who stuffed mashed cardboard into the exhaust..."

Dave was becoming increasingly interested.

"And what word did Annabel use?" She paused. "Hey, Dave. What word?" She did not wait for his response. "Nasty." She stared at him. "Quite a coincidence, huh?"

Detective Sergeant David Smith leapt out of bed.

"He's disguising himself," he shouted. "It wasn't a woman today, Luce. It was a man – for some reason targeting people who annoyed him by looking at their mobile phones."

"Or being slow at traffic lights," said Lucy.

"Or objecting to people who don't clear up after their dogs," he said.

He was searching for his clothes.

"Oh, fuck me, Luce. We've got a nutter loose," he shouted.

"He hasn't killed anyone yet, Dave," Lucy exclaimed.

"He will, Luce. He will. It's just a matter of time."

"What are you doing?"

Dave was getting dressed. "Going in."

"What, at three in the morning?" she asked.

"He's at it now, Luce. He's planning his next attack."

Milton Grant knew exactly what the police would be doing. They depended on repetition for much of their detective work. He wanted to avoid them, and also needed to clear his head. He had now completed three corrections, and worried that someone might connect the elderly woman in the supermarket car park to the other attacks. Stella never pressured him and so, when he called round to tell her he couldn't make Sunday lunch, she reacted with equanimity.

He just wished she wouldn't do that thing.

31

After confirming that she would see him the following Tuesday afternoon, they said their farewells.

Early on Friday morning he joined the M1, stopped on the M6 for breakfast, took the toll road round Birmingham, re-joined the M6 and sped past Manchester and Preston. After passing Kendal he took a left towards the eastern section of the Lake District. He reached his destination of Brothers Water, north of Windermere and south of Ullswater, around eleven o'clock. He found a comfortable hotel in the village of Hartsop, which meant 'the valley of the deer', booked in, showered, changed into his walking kit, ate three bananas and left to complete a twelve-mile hike in the four hours of daylight that remained.

He had found the small lake, once called Broad Water, some years earlier after he and his ex-wife had argued. He had walked out and disappeared for a week. The lake is best seen from the northern end of the Kirkstone Pass, but Milton discovered that its real wealth was to be discovered by walking and sliding over the rocky fells surrounding the shallow waters. At the peak, the path is precariously close to the edge of a sheer drop down the scree-laden slope.

He arrived back, exhilarated by the exercise. He rested in his room for a while then went down to the lounge bar, where he ordered suet pudding. He was reading a Lee Child novel: he relished the violence as Jack Reacher demolished a group of five Los Angeles thugs. Later, another guest came over. "My name's Ray," he said. They chatted for about an hour and Milton let slip that, in the morning, he planned to go for a twenty-mile walk. The man invited himself to join him. Milton was displeased, but said nothing.

They left on time, after breakfast, on a stunning autumn morning. Milton's companion said little for the first hour. When they reached the start of the climb up the side of the mountain, Milton was interested when Ray volunteered that he was the chief executive of a private logistics business. He then told him that he was gay and his partner was in New Zealand on business.

They stopped to consume packed lunches, provided by the hotel, and drink some water. They decided that they had seen no more than perhaps twenty hillwalkers during the morning. Milton was beginning to warm to the other man: Ray was informed and interesting. They talked about politics and Brexit. They were enjoying themselves. His companion described the British taxation system as the biggest con trick ever levied by any government anywhere in the world.

As far as Milton was concerned, Ray's opinion was compelling. Ray explained that the majority of British workers were trapped in the PAYE system. Their pay-as-you-earn remuneration suffered deductions at source of national insurance and income tax. That was for starters. HM Revenue & Customs had draconian powers to pry: pensions were taxed at source, capital gains were taxed following disclosure on the annual return (and a fine levied if the return is submitted one day late), and then virtually all free money spent was subject to value added tax at 20%.

"Then there is the ultimate abuse of us all: fuel tax." Ray continued without hesitation. "A litre of petrol is around £1.16. Excise duty is 57p. On top of that there is VAT at 20%." He laughed. "The cost of a litre of petrol is 40p. Fuel duty is 57p. VAT is 19p."

He stood up and walked a few paces before turning back. "I've done the maths, Milt. The tax rate on a litre of petrol is 190%. Fucking 190%, Milt."

He had only just started. "The Chancellor of the bleedin' Exchequer collects all this money so that six hundred and fifty MPs can have fabulous salaries, unlimited expenses, housing allowances, mouth-watering pensions, knighthoods, peerages and chairmanships of government quangos, most of which achieve fuck all." He paused for breath. "They have numerous outside jobs and sit in parliament for three days a week, for less than twenty-two weeks of the year."

They were now picking up their pace.

"One more fact about tax," Ray said, slightly out of breath. "If you survive all the deductions." He gasped as he stumbled on a rocky outcrop. "When you die, the taxman takes most of your money in inheritance tax. The Conservatives came up with the plan that, when you go to heaven, any remaining assets should pay for your health care. As you're dead, you're paying for something that has rather let you down. It's crackers, Milt."

"It's called democracy," said Milton, assessing the storm clouds on the horizon.

Ray stopped and looked at his hillwalking friend.

"Paying tax is for lemmings," he said.

Milton grimaced. He had difficulty in understanding the taxation rules and codes he was forced to follow, and he was baffled by the deductions made following his divorce and the split of assets. "So, you don't pay tax?" he asked his companion.

"Oh yes, I do," was the immediate response.

"There's a well-known code amongst us high earners. The best accountants will be able to keep your personal tax below 5% of total income." He walked ahead of Milton and then allowed his companion to catch him up. They passed three hikers who were heading towards Kirkstone Pass.

"Below 5%," mused Ray. "I earn around half a million a year." He hesitated. "That's between you and me, mate. I don't even pay 190% fuel tax. My car, when my driver is not around, is filled up from the pool pumps. HMRC call it 'benefits in kind' and try and tax you." He looked at Milton. "They'll get you, Milt, but not me." He puffed out his chest. "I'm smarter than those pricks," he said.

He had yet more to say on the subject. "If a worker is earning perhaps £40,000 annually, he will be paying around 55% in tax when all deductions, VAT and so on, are taken into account."

They walked on, and began to descend into the valley. The sun had disappeared behind the clouds coming in from the west. Milton was lost in thought. Eventually, without reducing his pace, he posed a question. "What about the morality of your position?"

"What the fuck's that to do with it?" snapped Ray. "You sound like a religious type. I employ over seven hundred people. They depend on me. That's my fucking moralistic position. I go to work and give all I have because I earn big money. I have a luxurious pad on a secure housing estate. I travel first class and stay in top hotels. I have my wealth managed for me, overseas. My driver brought me up here because I wanted a break. He'll collect me tomorrow afternoon. I get tickets to any sporting event in the world. I go to the O2 arena whenever I want. I have a private doctor and a personal dentist. Everything is paid for by the business. And Mr HMRC knows better than to come near me. I employ particularly nasty and expensive tax lawyers and accountants." He laughed. "Last year they got me a tax rebate."

They walked on. Suddenly, Ray stopped and turned to face Milton. "You know what's best about my life, Milton?" He laughed. "I'll tell you. I haven't a worry in the world." He laughed and tripped over a fallen branch.

They returned to the hotel and agreed to have dinner in their rooms. They met early the next morning for breakfast, and Milton found he was looking forward to their second walk together. He had tossed and turned as he recalled their discussion on tax and money. But Ray was proving good company. They shared an interest in politics and he knew his stuff about global warming. Milton made a note to go and see *An Inconvenient Sequel*, Al Gore's latest work on climate change. Ray asked few questions about Milton.

They set off in slightly chillier conditions and calculated that they would eat an early packed lunch at the top of High Hartsop Dodd. They walked for two hours without speaking, and then revisited the previous day's discussion about wealth creation.

"Milt," said Ray, as his new friend recoiled at the use of his shortened Christian name, "Maggie got it right. Labour is very good at spending other people's money."

Milton decided he was warming to Ray – a lovely man, he thought. His companion was uncomplicated, which Milton liked. He would remember these two days for some time. They finished their lunch and Ray moved to the edge of the precipice, stared down at Brothers Water far beneath them, and breathed the fresh air deep into his lungs.

"My father used to bring me here," he said.

Then Milton came up behind him and gave him a ferocious shove in the back. Ray didn't make a sound as he fell. His body bounced off the outcrops of rock and into the water below. There was a splash. Over the next hour his body began to sink. The thunder began later that afternoon, and it would be three days before the corpse resurfaced at the southern edge of Brothers Water.

"Should have paid your taxes," said Milton.

He returned to the hotel and settled his bill using a false credit card. The name of Monty Underhill would later mean nothing to the police. He made a point of asking the whereabouts of the man he had breakfasted with and who had not kept their lunchtime rendezvous in the hills. He left the hotel and stopped the car after about ten miles, where he dumped his walking clothes and changed the car number plates as he wanted to avoid being caught on the automatic number plate recognition system used by the police. The following day he would drive to Shoreditch, sell the vehicle for cash and buy a saloon, also for cash, take it back to his garage and change the number plates.

He got home late on Sunday night, showered, changed and settled into his office. He was exhilarated by the past three days, decided it was time for Chopin, and put on the appropriate CD. He took out his list and added *No. 4: paying taxes*. He would go into London the next day and see the Al Gore documentary. He would see Stella on Tuesday and

Thursday and prepare for correction number five on the list. This would take place on Friday. He looked forward to the challenge.

At this stage he could not afford to attract attention. Later, it would not matter. But, for now, the adrenalin rush of being in charge and hitting back was exhilarating. His wife and daughter had tried to order him around, suggesting his police boots should be kept in the garage. But it was his inability to convict the bad guys that he hated. There had been the driving case that had ended with the CPS lawyer calling him a moron and the woman thanking him for being a misogynist. He was a police officer who had been prevented from controlling people's bad behaviour – due to their fucking human rights. But Milton Grant was made of sterner stuff. He was getting revenge, making a difference – and he was loving it.

By unspoken consent, Lucy and Dave had ditched their post-marriage vow. Shop talk was now the order of the day. It was Sunday evening and they were seated at their dining room table, which was in an extension of the kitchen.

Lucy looked at her husband, nodded, bowed her head and closed her eyes. Dave opened the Bible and began to speak. "Saint Paul taught about tolerance. This is from Romans 14, verse 13." He coughed. "Therefore let us not judge one another anymore, but rather resolve this, not to put a stumbling block or a cause to fall in our brother's way."

Lucy mouthed "Amen" and stood up.

"Come on, Luce, what is it?"

"Hah," she laughed. "You know the choice of

four. If you get it right you will receive a special reward later."

Dave groaned with anticipation. "Hell, Luce, one out of four. The odds are weighted in your favour."

"Your choice, Dave. By the way, I went shopping yesterday."

He moaned inside and wondered if they could skip the meal – but he was hungry.

"Beef, pork, lamb or gammon," he said.

"Correct," she acknowledged. She hated chicken so never cooked it.

As he had looked in the oven an hour earlier, he knew the answer but decided to play up to his wife.

"Gammon," he chose.

"Lucy's the champion," she sang as she danced around the kitchen. She returned with a serving dish containing a rack of Welsh lamb, and took the lids off serving bowls full of roasted parsnip, carrot and cheese-covered cauliflower. Finally, blowing an imaginary trumpet, she revealed her pièce de résistance. Her roast potatoes were in a class of their own because her mother had taught her to sprinkle sugar over them every thirty minutes.

One of Lucy and Dave's relationship 'rules' was that, when their duty rosters allowed, they would have Sunday dinner together at seven in the evening. This went back to Lucy's childhood. As a child, Lucy and her brother had always sat down for dinner with their parents. Her father always read a passage from the Bible before they ate, and her mother always served a roast dinner. They talked together during and after the meal, and this family time was important to Lucy.

She was working hard to make her marriage a success: she had too many colleagues whose relationships were in trouble. She was determined that her marriage would not wither because of the lack of communication she detected in others. The other danger area was not a risk for them due to Dave's insatiable appetite for her.

Four months after their wedding they had gone to her parents' home for Sunday dinner. Dave started off well by giving her mother a bouquet of flowers, her father the latest Wilbur Smith novel and her brother a ticket for the next home game. They talked until after ten. On their way home, Lucy had suggested that they should adopt her parents' tradition of having Sunday dinner together. Much to her surprise Dave agreed, and said he wanted to start by reading from the scriptures. She had thought that the only God her husband worshipped was Arsene Wenger, closely followed by St Paul (aka Patrick Vieira).

Sunday dinner together became embedded into their lives. After Dave had read from the Bible, Lucy served the meal and Dave poured wine. Both police officers were on early shift the following morning, so they were limiting their alcohol intake.

"Dave?" asked Lucy.

"Yes, honey?" he replied before adding a further roast potato to his plate.

"You never do anything without there being a purpose to it," she said.

"Am I that obvious?" he laughed.

"The scripture reading you chose. About tolerance. Are you trying to tell me something?"

He put his knife and fork down and drank some wine. "We can't find the acid attacker. He's still out there, and my boss says it is only a matter of time before he kills someone. He's made the case a priority. We're under pressure to find him."

"Clues?" she asked. "I'm trying to think about tolerance."

"Well done, Luce. That's the path I'm treading." He drank some more wine.

"Could I have a herbal tea?" she requested.

He returned with their drinks.

"Right. This shit we're looking for objects to drivers who are slow to pull away from traffic lights, attacks people who fail to clear up after their pets, and sprays acid on people with mobile phones."

"So far. But this last week has been trouble-free," she said.

"Yes. So, he's a male around forty or fifty, he's about five foot eleven inches tall, he weighs around twelve stones, he's dark-haired and he's fit. That's what the clever lot tell me from their studying of the CCTV images."

"He's violent and he hates," said Lucy.

"Yes. He's intolerant of people's habits. Mobile phone users piss me off but I don't go around spraying acid on them."

"There's a sequence, Dave. Traffic lights, but no immediate physical assault, dog poo – and you saw what he did to the man in the park, and mobile phones, and he ruined a young woman's life. All we have to do is work out what he might do next."

"That's where I am, Luce. I'm preparing a list of what annoys other people."

"Can I help?" she asked.

"Shoot," ordered Dave.

"Where do I start?" She laughed. "Men who order me about."

"Interesting. There are four of us working on the case and both my female colleagues have come up with that one." He drank his coffee.

"Middle-lane hoggers," she said.

"Don't say that to traffic." Dave laughed. "They're sensitive to what they take as personal criticism."

There was no stopping Lucy. "People who eat with their mouth open," she suggested.

"People who eat in the street," said Dave. "My mum never let me do it."

"People who don't put their dustbins back after the council have emptied them," continued Lucy.

"Cyclists who use the pavement," suggested Dave.

They started to clear away the dinner plates.

"You know Alice, who I work with?" asked Dave.

"You mean the one with the big—"

"Yes, her," said Dave, as he pretended to smack his wife. "She came up with an interesting one."

"Men who don't have an erection when she enters the room," said Lucy, hiding playfully.

Dave began to wash up. Lucy grabbed a tea towel.

"She said that the thing that annoys her more than anything is elderly people who fumble at the supermarket till and take ages to pay their bill. They really—"

Lucy dropped a plate on the kitchen floor.

"Dave!" she cried. "Three weeks ago. An OAP who had delayed people at the checkout at the supermarket was assaulted – a hit and run – and we've got it on CCTV."

Stella lay back in the bath and allowed the warm water to ease the bruising between her legs. Milton had been quite loving on Tuesday but two days later he had acted like a man possessed. She smiled in satisfaction as she recalled the effect her suspenders and stockings had on him. He never spoke when they made love, but was always caring and attentive to her.

She relished the simplicity of their relationship. The rules were clear and acceptable to both parties. She wondered if it would ever end. If it did, she would move on. One of her ex-husbands was hounding her for money. The pretty assistant ten years his junior with whom he had set up home had run off with all his assets. "Hard fucking luck," had been Stella's unsympathetic response. The hot water was cooling, so she turned on the tap to top up the bath. She had milked her ex for all he had. Stella laughed. "Tee, hee, ha," was the sound that emerged from her mouth. "Tee, hee, ha." She always laughed in the same way. To Milton, it sounded like a cross between a five-year-old and a Chinese stand-up comedian. He wished she wouldn't laugh like that.

Milton was alone in his office at the end of an enjoyable Thursday. He was playing a Beethoven CD and preparing for correction number five. Tomorrow, in the evening, teenagers and twenty-somethings would descend on the town centre, where they would consume so much alcohol that a number would have to be taken to hospital. They would puke on the streets, they would fight each other, they would assault innocent pedestrians, they would throw bricks at cars, and the local press would photograph girls lying in the gutter with their mini-skirts up to their unmentionables. A few offenders would reach the magistrate's court where they would get a slap on the wrist.

Milton became interested in the behaviour of the young people. One fact he did discern was that 'binge drinking' was affected by the fact that the young people did not drink alcohol during the week. Many did not have the money. By the time Friday night came around, they were worked up in the expectation of escaping their dreary lives. They inflicted on their bodies an avalanche of alcoholic drinks. They would drink too much, they would be ill, some would take drugs and many would need medical help. The next week they would return for more.

Milton despised them. He thought they represented a decadent decline in society. They created havoc and damage. They didn't vote. They had never fought a war. They expected other people to look after their grandparents. They had no respect for authority.

In his early years as a police constable, it had been different. Some of his colleagues relished the fights and made sure that the bad guys were sorted out. Over a period of time, with the increasing use of CCTV and ambitious chief constables trying to make a name for themselves by favouring society against policing, things had changed. He hated it, and did all he could to avoid Friday night duties. When his efforts failed he resented the hours he spent in hospital corridors watching people fight and vomit.

Before his marriage ended he had a brief affair with a female officer. It was his usual style: pure sex. After an argument, she had stormed out of their hotel bedroom, leaving behind her uniform. She and Milton were a similar height. Even though the uniform was a few years old, it was perfect for his needs.

He stripped off and showered, then he shaved his

legs. He needed to think like a woman. Last week, he had bought white underwear, which he now put on. The blonde wig was perfect. He shaved his eyebrows, and he would shave his face an hour before going out. He put on the rest of the clothes and added the equipment carried by front-line officers, including pepper spray. He had rebuilt the boots and lowered them by an inch, and added deeper pockets at the top of the trousers to hold everything he needed. He spent four hours preparing for his evening out. Mitch Leary would have admired his performance. Milton was not going to try to kill the President – but he was intent on causing some serious damage.

The next day, he left his home by the side door. He had not eaten since lunchtime because of the need to be physically alert. He had surveyed the area many times and decided his chances of being seen were remote. In any case, no one was going to challenge a police officer. He covered the mile and a quarter into town in around forty minutes, ducking in and out of the shadows. He checked his watch, which he had bought in Poundland. It was clear faced with a pink strap. It was eleven fifty-two. His plan was to keep to the back streets until he reached the town centre, where the northern side of the square housed the war memorial and led into the park.

A number of blue lights flashed. There was an increased police presence following an unusually nasty fight. Milton was unaware that a small group of travellers had descended on a school playground and planned to stay there until council officials moved them on. Three of the travellers left their caravans and decided to drink in the town. The locals then decided to sort them out. This was a situation in which the police operated effectively. They arrived in force, made some arrests and restored order. Milton was frustrated. He would have preferred to handle the travellers himself.

The town centre was settling back to normal, with drinkers everywhere. He decided to keep to his plan and select three men and two women for correction. He kept to the shadows of the war memorial and watched two girls trying to light a cigarette. They were drunk, their clothing awry, and one had slumped over a concrete wall and seemed to be unconscious. Her friend was giggling and attempting to pull her upright.

Milton went behind her, put one hand over her mouth and pulled her away and into the entrance to the woods. His strategy was dependent on speed of action. Once the police realised there were multiple attacks taking place, they would close the area down. The woman was utterly confused, although she tried to fight off her attacker. She was on her back. She opened her mouth and gasped for air as he poured a mixture of washing-up liquid and bleach down her throat. He whispered in her ear, "Think before you drink, cretin."

He left her lying in the grass. After he had run about a hundred yards and exited the trees, he spotted two youths trying to fight each other but they were so drunk, it was a farce. Neither knew what had hit them when Milton repeated his corrective actions. He left them moaning in the undergrowth, kicking one on the head to give him a few more precious minutes to escape, then put his mouth to his ear. "Think before you drink, cretin."

He was pleasantly surprised to find, on re-entering the square, a young man on his own. Milton overpowered him and poured the liquid down his throat. The young man heard the same message.

Milton needed just one more victim. Then he spotted her. She was trying to hail a cab, but the driver drove straight past her. She shouted abuse after him. Before long Milton was dragging her behind a parade of shops. She heard a dog bark and somebody play loud music.

He squeezed her nose and held the last bottle of liquid over her mouth. He was worried about the time that had elapsed since his first attack, and wanted to complete the correction as quickly as possible. He was totally unprepared when she fought back. She scraped her nails down his face – and knew that she was fighting a man. Unusually, Milton was slow to react. When she grabbed his testicles and squeezed, his agony was enhanced by the shock of her resistance. He was slow and dulled by shock. He hit her on the side of the head. She lost consciousness, so she did not feel the kick he added for good measure.

Forty minutes later he was home. He entered by the side door, locked up, went into the kitchen and undressed, putting every item of clothing into two black bin liners. He showered, put on a tracksuit and went into his office. He had pre-selected a CD, which was ready to play. As a Mozart piano concerto filled the room, he slowly sank his head into his hands and shook with anger.

Stella spent some of Saturday evening in her hot tub, drinking too much wine. She was listening to Neil Diamond, who wanted to tell her about 'summer love'. Milton's telephone call had surprised her, and the prospect of no sex for a week was disappointing.

She kept to her self-imposed discipline of never asking questions: she would see him again a week on Tuesday. Perhaps her boss might give her a week's break. Then she remembered the patients who depended on her healing powers and decided against it. She would go to the cinema and see *Goodbye Christopher Robin*. She wiped a tear away as she recalled her mother reading Winnie the Pooh stories to her. She laughed as she remembered Tigger's antics. "Tee, hee, ha."

Lucy bowed her head as Dave read from the Bible.

"Matthew 6, verses 14 and 15," he began. "For if you forgive other people when they sin against you, your heavenly father will also forgive you. But if you do not forgive others their sins, your father will not forgive your sins."

She opened her eyes, went to the oven and took out a side of pork which she had already partly sliced. She then took out the potatoes and vegetables and a sauce. He poured the wine and they began to eat.

They were tired. The hunt for the mysterious attacker was proving abortive. Dave and Lucy had both had to work overtime, partly to reassure the public. The press naming the attacker 'The policewoman attacker' had not helped to calm things down.

All five victims were seriously ill after they had been forced to drink the mixture of liquid soap and bleach. Two recovered relatively quickly, as they had managed to spit much of the substance out. The girl who had been attacked first was the worst affected, and remained in intensive care.

"So," said Lucy. "You are suggesting we forgive

this bastard?"

"I was reading from the gospel according to St Matthew," replied her husband.

"How near are you to getting him?" she asked.

"We know a lot about him," replied Dave. "The image from the supermarket CCTV, thanks to you, was constructive. We have a pretty good idea now about his appearance. The girl who fought back saw him close up, and her Identikit picture has been helpful. We've plastered it everywhere and visited most homes in the area but nobody can identify him."

"He's gone to ground, hasn't he?" she asked.

"She also managed to scratch him. She got some skin – and his DNA – but we haven't been able to find a match. He's hiding."

"What does the profiler say?" she asked.

"What you would expect: the attacks are escalating, but he's following a pattern. The profiler thinks he will kill before very long. He needs to be found, but he also wants to make it as difficult for us as he can." Dave paused. "We call him 'the man who hates' in the office. The profiler has cautioned us about that. He says that everybody has hang-ups, especially motorists. We are all annoyed by the selfishness of mobile phone users." He stopped to spoon another roast potato onto his plate. "He suggests we concentrate on what has triggered his campaign. It doesn't seem to be sexual in any way, though. All his women victims have confirmed that there was absolutely no sign of that. You know, Luce – no ripping of clothing, or hands on breasts. And he had the opportunity."

"So," said Lucy, "he's not a sexual pervert."

"We've checked everyone with a record of sexual

deviance, rapists and paedophiles to a radius of twenty miles. We've arrested two people as a result, but neither is the man we want."

"If he's not a sexual predator, that suggests he's sexually satisfied," she said.

"Yes," he said cautiously, "it's generally accepted that rapists are on a power trip – that raping is not sexually motivated."

"Let me finish, Dave, and stop interrupting me," she said.

"Go on," encouraged Dave, enjoying his wife being on her own power trip.

"So, I think he's happily married."

"Unlikely, Luce." Dave poured them each another glass of wine. "Can you see him managing to perfect his disguises and arrive back with scratches on his face without a wife or partner noticing?"

"Oh yes. Time to rethink. So maybe he's a loner. I still think you might be missing something."

Dave frowned but said nothing.

"OK, Dave, sorry," she said. "I'll leave the detective work to you."

"Go on, Luce," said Dave. "Sorry, honey. I was out of order."

"You're tired, Dave." She went round to him and sat by his side.

"One piece of Lucy detection and then you're going to bed." She kissed him and then poured him a whisky. He grabbed the glass.

"He knows too much, Dave." She sipped her glass of elderflower. "He's here in our midst. I just don't believe he's coming in and out of town. Anyway, he was at the supermarket shopping. I think he's local."

"OK," said Dave.

"We've had no success on the ANPR system, so we think he's changing his number plates. He's disguising himself. That's not easy, but he knows what features matter. His skin is different each time, according to the witnesses. That's smart." She marshalled her thoughts. "He seems to know too much. Take the Friday night bleach attacks. He knew where we would be. But there's not one police officer who can recall seeing him. No CCTV caught him. He was wearing a policewoman's outfit and would have stood out a mile at around six foot. Nobody saw him. And where did he get the uniform? We've visited the fancy dress shops and nobody has handled one for months." Lucy laughed. "We did find a strip-o-gram who does a policewoman act, but she starts off wearing so little in the first place."

The introduction of levity lifted their discussion. Dave yawned.

"So," said Lucy, "do you want me to solve the case?"

"What's keeping you, Luce?" laughed her husband.

"He's a former police officer," said Lucy.

"Say that again?"

Thirty minutes earlier Milton had looked down into the toilet bowl at the black blood. He knew that the end was not too far away.

Now, he lay back in his office chair and absorbed the preludes of his favourite French composer. He and Claude Debussy had one thing in common: rectal cancer. The maestro had chosen to have a colostomy which had failed to prolong his life, and he had succumbed at the age of fifty-five. Milton had ignored the bleeding until, eventually, he had no choice but to see a doctor. He did not even consider the operation he was offered. He had no one to look after him and, in truth, nobody to live for. His ex-wife had moved away and his daughter Jennifer rarely contacted him, not even to acknowledge receipt of her monthly allowance. This year, for the first time, she had missed his birthday.

After his diagnosis, he had spent nearly three weeks walking in the Pyrenees deciding his future. A combination of suppositories, and a drug prescribed by the surgeon, held the cancer temporarily at bay. He even managed to bed a hotel guest, like Edward Fox in *The Day of the Jackal* when he seduced the countess, later murdering her, but Milton had simply moved on. He found it frustrating that the oncologist couldn't give a definitive answer to his obvious question. Instead he gave a rather bland reply: "Let's say between seven and twelve months."

Milton reflected on his parting of the ways with the police force. He recognised that he had been lucky to have an Assistant Chief Constable who understood the circumstances of the event that had resulted in his disciplinary hearing. It was, in his mind, ludicrous. He had been called to a dispute in a charity shop. Two people were arguing over purchasing rights to a dress: neither would give way. Each claimed to have been the first to want to buy it. The elderly assistant panicked and called the police. When Milton arrived, the two aggressors were squaring up to each other. The sight of Milton propelled them into violence. As he attempted to part them, one, whose hair was dyed orange, deliberately (in his opinion) poked Milton in the eye. He should never have said what he did, but he did.

"You fat lump of lard," he had cried out.

The two pugilists stopped in mid-fight.

"Did you hear what he said?" one asked the other. "Who's he calling fat?" She then shouted at her two children, who were spreading jigsaws over the floor.

Milton had got on his radio to ask for assistance. His eye was now closed and rather painful. From there on, the situation escalated out of his control. Both ladies were obese. Their years of eating burgers, chips and chocolate were reflected in their dress size – which was the cause of the fracas. Neither would admit it, but they found it hard to buy clothes that fitted.

Milton was taken to hospital. The two women both put in formal complaints, the shop assistant said that she couldn't remember what had happened, and the more heavily built complainant accused Milton of inflicting his eye injury himself to deflect attention from the words he had used. They were both after money – and that is what they received. Milton was appalled at the amount they were paid. The Assistant Commissioner told him to accept a formal reprimand. When Milton hinted at taking early retirement, the senior officer made it straightforward for him. Milton was out of the force three months later.

Initially, he was lost. He enrolled at the local college to study music, but did not mix well with the younger students. He maintained his fitness regime but noticed that he was struggling to finish his six-mile runs. His diagnosis changed everything. He had a short-term purpose in life. He found Stella and settled down to plan his list. Before he died, he would apply correction to eight groups of people he hated.

The supermarket incident was a bonus. He had

now completed five of the eight actions, and he knew what the last would be. He could hardly wait. After the girl in the market square had fought back, he knew the police would find him. But first, he had three tasks to complete. He completed the sixth with relative ease. Milton hated Irish travellers. To him, they were scum. When he watched the news item about three caravans in a school car park and the disruption to the school, after a day tending his face, he went out late at night and placed an incendiary device under the first mobile home. The bomb exploded. Of the seventeen people on the site, three received serious burns, one broke a leg jumping out of her caravan doorway, and two suffered smoke inhalation. Other travellers arrived to take them all away to a new site. A council officer arrived and pinned an eviction notice to the last remaining caravan.

Milton was pleased that correction number seven was under way. He had selected the retail outlet. He recoiled at modern eating habits, because, in his opinion, wherever he went, people were pigging themselves. In the cinema they spoilt his enjoyment by munching noisily through huge boxes of popcorn and slurping giant cups of coke. Some managed to spread the cheese covering their nachos all over the seats. In the streets he watched as they ate burgers, chips, chicken nuggets, ice cream, crisps and more. They would then expect the medical world to sort out their polluted insides and wrecked joints. They were the first to complain when they could not get a doctor's appointment. They blamed immigrants, and argued that their own benefits payments were too low.

He had found a food outlet where the meat was delivered early in the morning in a secure refrigerated van. He had followed the delivery van several weeks earlier and now knew when the driver would stop for his morning coffee. He took from the back of the unlocked vehicle a parcel of meat which he took home and refrigerated. Last night he had injected the meat with a poison he had bought on the internet. He calculated it would be enough to poison about twenty people – they would experience an agonising intestinal disorder. Early that morning he had waited until the driver went in for his coffee and slipped the package into the back of his van. Two days later, the local A&E was overwhelmed with patients, all of whom were vomiting blood.

Milton Grant was left with one final correction. He could not wait to begin.

Lucy read the text message she'd just received from Dave. She was on enquiries and had been dealing with a mother whose daughter had been missing overnight. Lucy had been baffled that, when the mother handed her a photograph of her daughter, she had apologised that her daughter was rather overweight.

Dave's text read:

He's Milton Grant. He lives on the north side. We're going in. Luv u x

Lucy decided not to return the text. "Please remember, Dave," she said to herself, "he's dangerous."

To hell with protocol, she thought next. *Luv u 2*, she texted.

The police cordoned off the area and the armed unit went in. Another group raided Milton's garage.

Inside the house they found everything they needed. There was enough evidence to send him to prison for life. They discovered his disguises. They read his medical notes and letters. They had all they required to close down the man who hated. There was just one problem. Milton Grant was nowhere to be seen.

Pinned to the kitchen wall was a note.

Late again, lads. Hope the fatties did not delay you.

He had rented the flat as a potential bolthole three months earlier. He calculated the police would find him within forty-eight hours. That gave him enough time to do what he had planned. He lay low for a day and then went to see Stella for the last time.

She had purchased a fresh set of underwear and cleaned the Jacuzzi. She did not ask any questions, although she noticed the marks on his skin. She watched his face as he savoured the incense and watched as she slowly slid her skirt up her thighs. When he saw her black knickers, he exploded with passion. He took her to bed. He was brutal during sex, and hurt her.

When he was preparing to leave, Stella noticed a grey hair in his head and pulled it out. "Tee, hee, ha," she laughed.

He circled behind her, took out a knife and pulled it savagely across her throat. Blood spurted from her carotid artery. He let her body slump to the floor.

"I wish you didn't do that," he said.

Lucy knew that Dave was tired. The message Milton Grant had left in the kitchen had upset him. She mused over his words: *Hope the fatties did not delay you.* They went to bed early as they were both on early duty the next day. The next morning an elderly man came into the police station to report his wife missing. She was diabetic. Her husband was worried because she had not returned home the previous evening from a walk in the park. Lucy blinked when she looked at the photograph he had brought with him.

Milton began the final stage of his corrective campaign by completing a two-mile run, showering, enjoying a bowl of bananas and peaches, and putting on a casual outfit. He left the flat with a handkerchief and chloroform in his pocket, reached the disused warehouse and entered through the back door. He switched on the lights and checked his two prisoners.

The first was the girl of nineteen. She was naked and her hands were tied behind her back. The rope was attached to a bracket Milton had previously hammered into the wall. She had a gag around her mouth. Her eyes reflected her fear. Urine and excrement dribbled down the inside of her legs. She was heavy, with rolls of fat around her stomach, a large bottom, and breasts hanging painfully without the support of a bra.

The other victim was the elderly diabetic woman. She was semi-conscious. She was also heavy, but not as heavy as the young woman. She was tied up in exactly the same way and was also naked. Milton prodded them both and pinched the young woman's stomach. Her screams were muffled by the gag.

"Now, ladies," said Milton, "You are both very fat. You are selfish – because you expect me and my fellow taxpayers to cough up for all the medical treatment you require." He stood up and hit them with a stick. He was loving this moment of fulfilment.

"You drink to excess and you stuff processed foods into your mouth all day long. You block our buses because your arse is too large to fit into a seat. We can't get appointments at the doctors because you are there needing pills to treat a multitude of illnesses as a result of your self-inflicted obesity. The chemists are overworked because you need so many pills." He wiped his mouth. "It's because all you do is push food into your huge mouth all day."

He then took out a whip. He turned the women around so they were facing the wall and gave them each five lashes on their buttocks, which wobbled under the impact.

"When you leave here, I want you both to turn over a new leaf: You will stop eating to excess. Right, I'm going out now. When I return, I'll talk to you some more."

He turned them round, ignoring the stench. He was enjoying himself. He left the building and went out into the park. He spotted her within five minutes. A woman in her twenties was running and then stopping to do push-ups. Her colour offset her white kit. She was perfect for his needs. He went up to her to congratulate her on her fitness. Initially, the athlete was suspicious, but he seemed a pleasant man and quite fit himself. When she briefly turned her back on him, he put one arm round her throat and with the other held the handkerchief, which he had soaked in chloroform, to her mouth and nose. After fifteen seconds, she had stopped struggling.

He dragged her to the warehouse, where he stripped off her clothes and tied her to the bracket by his other two prisoners. The gag prevented her from screaming. She was fit – an athlete, a javelin thrower.

Her coach thought she had a chance of making the Olympics in Japan in 2020. Her black skin glowed with health. Despite her punishing training regime, however, she was overeating. Her coach had warned her that she was jeopardising her future in the team. Milton looked at her naked body. Because of her relative youth, it was tantalising.

Lucy looked up from reading Dave's latest text message.

We can't find him x

Inspector Sanderson was passing through reception when he spotted DC Avril Wren.

"Avril," he shouted. "I've lost my bloody javelin thrower. She was due here forty-five minutes ago."

Lucy knew that in his spare time the inspector ran the local athletics club.

"She's probably having a burger, guv," said DC Wren. "You need to get her to lose some weight."

"She'll be in the park. Pop down and find her, will you? The coach leaves in an hour."

Lucy ignored this misuse of police time and concentrated on what she had just heard. She pulled out a local map and studied the area around the park. She was thinking through what she knew. There was a missing girl aged nineteen who lived on the north side. There was a missing diabetic woman who lived on the south side. There was an athlete who had been in the park but who was now potentially missing. Lucy sidled over to Inspector Sanderson.

"Have you seen a rather strongly built javelin thrower?" he asked, laughing.

"No, guv," replied Lucy. "You know this area pretty well. Can you think of a building that's secluded where you could hold people?"

"You mean like my missing athlete?" he said

"No, guv," she said. "Just something I'm following up on."

He thought carefully.

"There's the parade of shops on the east side before the motorway link. The area is derelict – the owner is trying to get rid of all the tenants then knock the block down and sell the land for redevelopment. Fifty flats, I think. There's a disused store room behind the building which he also wants to demolish. Must go. Bloody javelin throwers," he added.

It was almost time for Lucy's lunch break. She collected her hat and decided to walk down to the area the inspector had identified. Twenty minutes later, she arrived. There was a side entrance which was locked. She went round to the front and managed to push open the door. She peeped through the crack and saw the three women. Lucy gasped, but knew what she had to do. She stepped back and used her radio to call the duty sergeant. She then ignored the instructions she was given, went back to the front door, paused, took a deep breath and then put her shoulder to the door. Much to her surprise, it opened quite easily and she stumbled into the warehouse. Milton was talking to the bound and gagged prisoners. The smell was overpowering. He turned and started to walk towards her.

"Sent a child, have they?" he sneered.

"It's over, Milton," said Lucy. "I'm going to help these three ladies and you can wait for the cavalry. They'll be here in a few moments."

He reached into his back pocket and pulled out a gun. He pointed it at Lucy.

"I can't allow that," he said. "You take another step and I'll fire."

"If you must," said Lucy. She was clenching every muscle in an attempt to disguise her trembling.

She then heard the sirens of police cars and ambulances growing louder. Three officers, followed by a plain clothes detective, burst through the front door.

"Armed police!" came a cry.

A shot rang out.

The bullet penetrated his jaw and smashed his brain into smithereens. He was dead before he hit the ground. Lucy stepped up and kicked the gun away. She then rushed to the three victims and spotted a pile of blankets which she grabbed. She hugged the young woman. She covered her in a blanket and whispered words of comfort into her ear. The diabetic lady was semi-conscious. The javelin thrower shrugged off her experience, saying she still had time to reach the coach and take part in the athletics tournament.

Lucy was covered in dirt. She looked up. Three armed policemen were staring at her. There was also a plain clothes officer.

"Dave," said Lucy. "We need to have a chat about your time-keeping."

Quickly, the paramedics took over. The young woman was in a bad condition and was quickly taken away for treatment. The elderly lady was delirious. Despite a huge effort by the medical team, she never regained consciousness. The athlete was back to normal within minutes and, after wrapping several blankets around her, managed to persuade an officer to take her home. She said that after she had changed she'd go to the police station.

"Luce," said Dave. "Are you all right? By the way, you smell awful."

"Take me home, Dave," she said. "I need a long, hot shower."

The elderly lady died seven hours later. Her family was by her bedside, including two of her four grandchildren. Her husband never recovered and passed on three months later.

Milton Grant's body was taken to the mortuary. On the gurney next to him was the body of a middle-aged woman who had had her throat cut.

A day later, during a squally shower of rain, a letter was delivered to Milton Grant's house. The postman rarely visited. Because of the police tape, he threw the letter into the porch. The on-duty officer, who had been checking the back of the house, trod on the letter. It somehow became part of the rubbish which was eventually cleared away by council workers. Had Milton opened his post, he would have read the following:

Dear Dad,

Yes, sorry and all that. I should have written. Happy birthday.

THANK YOU, THANK YOU, THANK YOU for the money. I can't exist without it.

Mum has started talking about you again. She's fine. She's seeing a new bloke. He's OK. She says I should try to rebuild our relationship. She keeps bringing up how good-looking you were (sorry, whoops, are) and how she loved the hillwalking you did together. She was proud of you and your career as a copper.

I didn't want to tell you this, but I'd better. I had a bit of bother with the police. Only soft stuff, but I got dragged in front of the court. I was let off, thank God. I've enrolled at a local college to do media studies. I'd like to be a Sky News presenter.

Dad, can we be friends?

Love you.

Jenny

"Please take a seat, Police Constable Smith," instructed Inspector Sanderson.

Lucy sat down opposite her boss.

"You disobeyed orders," he said.

"Yes, guv."

"You were told to await the arrival of the armed unit."

"Yes, guv."

"You went in, against orders," he continued.

"Yes," said Lucy.

"You risked your life."

"Yes, guv," she replied. "That was my choice."

Inspector Sanderson looked askance at her. "He had a gun."

"I didn't know that," said Lucy.

"You risked your life," repeated the inspector.

"I saw the three victims. They were in real trouble. I had to reach them." She hesitated. "May I have some water?"

The senior officer poured her water.

"If officers go around making up the rules, the force collapses, PC Smith. I can't allow it to happen."

"No, guv. I understand that."

"You are off on a week's holiday, I understand."

"Yes. Dave and I have got the press all over us. We're flying out tonight to Spain."

"Lucy, make me a promise," said Inspector Sanderson. "In future, you'll obey orders."

"No, guv," Lucy replied. "If I see someone needing a copper, I'll respond."

"Yes." He smiled. "I knew it was pointless asking." He stood up. "Go and enjoy your break."

Lucy stood up and walked towards the door.

"Detective Constable Smith," said her boss.

She stopped in her tracks and turned.

"There will also be a citation, Lucy. You saved two lives. We think that the pile of blankets were for wrapping up the bodies. We're pretty certain he was going to kill them. The elderly lady was gone anyway."

"Thank you, sir."

She turned and began again to head out of his office.

"Lucy," he said. "The javelin thrower made it to the competition."

She looked back. Her face was a picture of professional fulfilment. "That's great, sir."

"She came third." He smiled.

Their plane was late leaving and they arrived on the Costa Brava at well past midnight. At their hotel, they went straight to bed. The following morning they woke early and decided to go for a walk along the beach. The morning was still cool, but it was better than being at home – and there was not a reporter in sight.

"Detective Constable Smith," said her husband.

"You're still superior to me," laughed Lucy.

"Was that in any doubt?" replied Dave as he pinched her bottom.

She giggled.

"But Lucy," he chided. "Inspector Sanderson was right. You shouldn't have gone in there by yourself. I was worried about you."

"I like to live dangerously," teased Lucy.

"Oh, since when?" he asked.

"I married you, didn't I?"

On a bitterly cold November afternoon in a North London cemetery, Milton Grant was buried in a grave with a plain headstone. There was a brief inscription recording his name and dates. The only additional words were *Father of Jenny*. Jennifer and her mother held hands. Detective Constable Lucy Smith was also there. The minister read a few verses from the Bible and then hurried away.

Milton would have approved of that. He hated fuss.

THE END

FALLING DOWN: THE FILM

The 1993 film starred Michael Douglas as William Foster, a divorced, unemployed engineer. His car vanity plate read 'D-Fens', suggesting an angry white male. His wife had a restraining order to keep him away from their daughter.

In a heatwave, Foster is caught in a Los Angeles traffic jam on his way to his daughter's birthday party. He starts to walk, and commences a rampage across the city. He trashes a convenience store and seizes a knife from two thugs. They chase him with a gun, which he secures for himself together with other weapons. He shoots into a ceiling in a restaurant.

The disintegration of Douglas's character reflects the racial tensions in 1990s LA. He is chased by Sergeant Prendergast, who is working his last day as a law enforcement officer. The film climaxes at Venice Pier where Prendergast confronts Foster, who pretends to draw a weapon. It is, in fact, a plastic water pistol. However, Prendergast shoots him dead.

Towards the end of the film there is one of the great lines in American cinema. William Foster does not comprehend what he has done. He asks: "I'm the bad guy?"

This sentence defines the movie and its meaning.

Falling Down was filmed with the backdrop of the 1992 Los Angeles riots, following the police shooting of Rodney King.

The film was a box office success. The distinguished American screenwriter, John Truby, called it 'an anti-Odyssey story about the lie of the American dream'. On the twenty-fifth anniversary of its release, April Wolfe wrote in *LA Weekly*: 'It remains one of Hollywood's most overt yet morally complex depictions of the modern white victimisation narrative.'

The director Joel Schumacher, now 78, is a US cinema great. His films include *The Client* (1994), *A Time to Kill* (1996), *Phone Booth* (2002) and *Blood Creek* (2009).

Michael Douglas is an all-time acting legend whose life reflects many of the characters he has played.

ALSO BY TONY DRURY

Sarah Rudd City Thriller series

Megan's Game: getBook.at/Megan

The Deal: getBook.at/Deal

Cholesterol: getBook.at/TDCholesterol

A Flash of Lightning: getBook.at/Lightning

The Lady Who Turned: getBook.at/TheLady

Sarah Rudd stories

On Scene and Dealing: the early career of DCI Sarah
Rudd   getBook.at/OSAD

Journey to the Crown: the Career of DCI Sarah Rudd
from 2003 – 2008   getBook.at/Journey2crown

Sarah Rudd Short Stories

The Contract Killer: getBook.at/CKiller

The Killer Who Missed: getBook.at/killerwhomissed

Stories written for HEART UK – The Cholesterol Charity. (All publisher's profits are paid to the charity)

Hannah's Choice

Joanna's Choice: getBook.at/JoannasChoice

Mark's Choice: getBook.at/MarksChoice

The Dinner Party

The Novella Nostalgia Series

Lunch with Harry: getBook.at/LunchHarry

Twelve Troubled Jurors: getBook.at/TwelveTJ

Forever on Thursdays
 getBook.at/foreveronthursdays

THE NOVELLA NOSTALGIA SERIES

This publishing initiative brings together the uniqueness of the novella and various memorable movies from the history of cinema.

The word 'novella' comes from the Italian for 'novel.' It has been interpreted in various ways including 'a long short story' or a 'short novel'. It can be traced back to the early renaissance in Italy and France. Giovanni Boccaccio wrote 'The Decameron' in 1353. This comprises 100 tales of ten people fleeing the black death. It was not until the 18th and 19th centuries that the novella emerged as a literary genre.

In 1941, the Austrian novelist Stefan Zweig wrote 'The Chess Novella' which was later renamed 'The Royal Game'. This was the inspiration for the 1960 film 'Brainwashed'.

Most modern novellas are published by Penguin Modern Classics. The various novella prizes seem to stipulate a word count of between 7,500 and 40,000. A key feature of the novella is its limited punctuation. There are no chapter headings and no breaks apart from spaces where the author needs to show a scene change.

-0-

'Lunch with Harry' pays tribute to one of the great films produced by Hollywood. Made in 1961, *'Breakfast at Tiffany's'* was based on the novella written by Truman Capote. It produced a mesmeric performance by Audrey Hepburn.

The modern tale is transferred to London and

features the charismatic Ella van Houten and Harry, who is guilt ridden following the death of his wife. They meet in Regent Street in unusual circumstances. Their growing relationship parallels their search for a model of the Mexican general, Santa Anna, who burned 'The Alamo' to the ground.

The second publication, is **'Twelve Troubled Jurors'** with echoes of '*12 Angry Men*' which gave the film world one of Henry Fonda's greatest performances.

This is followed by **'Forever on Thursdays'** which hints at the unforgettable British film '*Brief Encounter*'. The love affair between Celia Johnson and Trevor Howard remains an icon in film history.

-0-

Full details of the Novella Nostalgia series can be found at www.cityfiction.co.uk

If you would like to be notified when the next book is released, be sure to sign up for my free newsletter at:

tonydruryemailsign-up.gr8.com

ABOUT TONY DRURY

Tony is the author of five DCI Sarah Rudd City thrillers. In each, he draws upon his career as a London financier to expose the underworld of dark practices and shadowy characters. None, however, are able to withstand the bravery and incisive detection methods of one of the police force's bravest officers. Her juggling of career demands, husband, children and her own demons, make riveting reading.

He has now written two more novels which trace the early career of probationary police constable Sarah

Whitson. In 'On Scene and Dealing' she meets her future husband Nick. In 'Journey to the Crown' she has a devastating affair with Dr Martin Redding. The final chapter jumps ahead to sample her future life as a private detective.

Tony has created an innovative series as a novella writer. Reflecting iconic cinema classics, his first is 'Lunch with Harry', which is inspired by 'Breakfast at Tiffany's'. Others to follow include 'Twelve Troubled Jurors' (echoing '12 Angry Men') and 'Forever on Thursdays' (capturing the drama of 'Brief Encounter').

He writes short-stories wherein the net proceeds go to HEART UK – The Cholesterol Charity. He is an ambassador for the charity.

Aged seventy-one, Tony is a follower of the wisdom of Albert Einstein: "When a man stops learning, he starts dying." He lives in Bedford with his wife Judy. They value every trip down the M1 to Watford to be with Grandson Henry.

Connect with Tony online:
(e) tony@cityfiction.co.uk
(w) tonydrury.com
Twitter: mrtonydrury
Facebook: facebook.com/tony.drury.author
Goodreads: goodreads.com/TonyDrury